# Terror at Deadwood Lake

Lane Walker

## Other books in the Hometown Hunters Collection

*The Legend of the Ghost Buck*
*The Hunt for Scarface*
*The Boss on Redemption Road*
*The Day It Rained Ducks*
*The Lost Deer Camp*

*Terror at Deadwood Lake*
by Lane Walker


ISBN 978-0-9853548-4-8
For Worldwide Distribution
Printed in the U.S.A.

The Hometown Hunters Collection

www.lanewalkerbooks.com

*To all those who chase*
*their dreams and keep the faith.*
*All my love to my family and friends*
*who continue to support & inspire me.*
*An extra special thanks to my wife*
*and daughters who bring me*
*constant joy and happiness.*
*Keep hunting your dreams!*

# ~ 1 ~

Darkness.

I was completely surrounded by total blackness, and I was quickly running out of air. Each breath felt like my last!

Was I dead? Not yet at least. I gasped hard and managed to steal a little more oxygen. My chest made a loud heaving sound, searching for more air. But there wasn't much to get.

Then I remembered. *The bear—where is he?*

I tried to move but couldn't. It felt like I was buried alive, drowning in quicksand. I was in the middle of a real-life nightmare!

I quickly remembered the avalanche. I tried to shout but couldn't. The only sound that I could muster was a low groan.

In my mind I was yelling, "Help! Dad, where

are you?" but I couldn't even manage to move my mouth.

Suddenly I heard something. At first I thought it was my dad, but it wasn't.

It was *him!* I heard his deep, bellowing roar. There was no mistaking it. It was the huge brown bear we had been hunting.

Only now the tables had turned. We were no longer hunting him—he was hunting me! I couldn't move. I was trapped.

I knew hunting in Alaska could be dangerous, but I never expected this.

I never expected that I'd become the hunted!

# ~ 2 ~

Growing up in Alaska, I experienced cold like in no other place in the U.S. In fact, on many wintry days the temperature stays well below freezing. That's fine with me because I love the cold weather.

Our family enjoys hunting and fishing, and Alaska provided plenty of both. Hunting is something my dad and I really like to do together.

Dad is an avid hunter; he takes it seriously. He has hunted all over the world from Canada to Africa. I love listening to his hunting tales from when he was younger.

Hunting is more of a lifestyle for us than a hobby. It's all our family has ever known. On our property, we enjoy small game, deer, and moose. We live on Kodiak Island in a small town named Bolton, located between Kodiak and Old Harbor.

The scenery is amazing and world-famous. The mountains are majestic and the streams some of the purest in the world.

Our family wasn't native to Alaska. My dad grew up in Michigan and met my mom at college. Living in Michigan allowed him a lot of outdoor time. After Mom graduated with her teaching degree, they took off for the wilds of Alaska.

The first thing they did was buy a fishing boat. Dad knew that he'd need a boat to make money to live on in Alaska. They scraped together enough to buy a boat that wasn't anything spectacular, but it was enough for them to get started in the commercial fishing business. That's how the *Lil' Carpathia* came to be part of our family.

When Dad let Mom name the boat, she explained to him why she chose such an unusual name.

Mom loved history and one of her favorite areas was American history. As a little girl, she would sit and listen to her grandparents talk about how they had come to America as immigrants straight from Ireland. She loved their tales of traveling the seas and the adventures in the new land.

Her favorite story was about the *Titanic*. She always listened intently to her grandma talk about the *Titanic* and how the ship was thought to be unsinkable, a modern wonder of engineering at that time.

It was the tragic events of April 15, 1912 that helped name our family's fishing boat. That night the *Titanic* hit an iceberg, causing it to sink and drown more than 1,500 people.

For hours, the survivors thought all hope was lost and they would die at the hands of the mighty sea. But more than 700 survivors were rescued around four in the morning by a ship that had received the *Titanic*'s distress signal. That ship's name was the *Carpathia*.

To my mom, the name held a simple meaning of hope. The rescue was always her favorite part of the story because it came two hours after the Titanic had gone down and when all hope seemed lost. Mom had hoped the fishing boat would help her and Dad be able to enjoy the wilderness way of life they both wanted for their family. When it came time for her to inscribe the name on the bow, she grabbed a brush full of black paint and wrote *Lil' Carpathia* on it.

# ~ 3 ~

It was late May, and we were gearing up for my high school graduation. I'd been spending a lot of time with my dad getting the *Lil' Carpathia* ready for the fishing season. Baseball playoffs had just ended so we were making plans for a couple long fishing trips after graduation.

Dad and I had hunted and fished all around Alaska and the Midwest. Blacktail deer and coastal black bears were my favorites to hunt. I'd been fortunate enough to have taken several large black bears and actually had one full-mounted for Christmas the year before.

My post-graduation plans were set. I was going to stay home and take classes at the community college while learning the family fishing business. Education was important to our family, especially my mom. During high school, I took my grades as seriously as I took sports. My mom and dad always told me that school was my job and I'd better do my best.

Whether on the football field or during a math test, I always tried to do well. I'm very competitive and have always wanted to win, something my parents instilled in me since I was a young boy.

My dad would always say, "Dré, you're a Brown, and Browns never quit!"

My real name is André, but everyone calls me Dré. My full name is actually André Adam Brown II, my dad being the first André Adam Brown. The funny thing is that even though we have the same names, no one ever calls us by them. People call my dad Duke. Although there were many stories of how he got the nickname, no one knows for sure, but he's been called Duke since elementary school days.

I was the only child in our family. At first it was great; but as I got older, I always wished I had a brother or sister.

My parents' plan to fix my loneliness was to

buy me a dog, a chocolate Lab I named Major, and he quickly became one of my closest friends. We've had all kinds of adventures together. He loved hunting, and one of his favorite activities was to go after ducks on the local lakes. When we weren't hunting, we were exploring the mountains around our house.

Even though I grew up on Kodiak Island and hunted all my life, there was one animal I dreamed about hunting for years: the Kodiak brown bear. They aren't your average bears—they're some of the biggest ones on earth.

Seeing a brown bear is awesome. I'd seen plenty of them from a distance when I was young but had never gotten too close. Dad and I would set up camp on nearby Casper Mountain, a couple miles outside Bolton. We'd spend the night in a tent and cook our supper over a campfire. The next morning we'd sit and scope the nearby hills with our binoculars, spotting big brown bears coming out of hibernation. This was an annual event for us, and something I always looked forward to.

But every time I asked Dad about hunting one, he always said the same thing.

"Son, when it's your time to chase the great brown bear, you'll know."

Every year we went, and every year I got the same response from Dad. To hunt a Kodiak brown bear is most hunters' dream in Alaska. I was chomping at the bit to follow my dad into the deep mountains and hunt what I considered to be the ultimate predator.

The brown bear is the measuring stick for other big game animals. The unique thing about these bears is that most of the time they are the hunter, not the hunted.

The Kodiak brown bear has taken many hunters' lives. Our family came to know this only too well after a brown bear almost took my dad's life. Four years ago, Dad was hunting a huge one when he was attacked and barely survived.

In fact, if it wasn't for the trusty .357 Magnum he carried, he probably wouldn't have made it back. In the fight with the beast, Dad managed to get off a couple of shots with his pistol. The second one startled the bear and scared it off, saving Dad's life. I actually didn't know a lot of details about the day of the attack. Most of what I knew I'd overheard my mom telling people shortly after it happened.

Dad was bleeding and injured, and Mad Mike, his guide and bush pilot, carried him the two miles back to camp. From there they used a satellite phone and called in a medical helicopter to fly him out of the bush to the nearest hospital, more than two hundred miles away.

On the way there, Dad's heart stopped twice because he'd lost so much blood. I remember him telling Mom one night how he could hear the pilots praying because it didn't look good.

Thankfully Dad survived. But to this day, he carries a five-inch scar across his face and also walks with an unmistakable limp. He never complains though.

That was a day he would never forget and one that he seldom talked about. In fact, I'd never heard his account of the story. I wanted to know firsthand what it was like to be so close to a big bear like that. But it was too hard for him to talk about it. It was something he woke up every day trying to forget.

A Kodiak brown bear will show any human how quickly the tide can change, how quickly the hunter can become the hunted.

# ~ 4 ~

There was a big part of me that both feared and loved the great brown bears of Kodiak Island.

I've always craved adventure. I'm the one who dares to push the limits to see how far I can take something. I was always the first one to jump off the swings or do something crazy.

Many times when I was in elementary school, the office called home to tell my parents about another serious bump or bruise I'd gotten during recess. The worst was when I climbed to the top of the big slide and jumped off it on a dare from my one of my buddies, Billy Sanders.

That stunt didn't end too well because I broke both ankles. I was in casts the entire summer before fourth grade. It was horrible, but the jump did make me a legend at Bolton Elementary School.

Through elementary and high school I divided all my energy between two things—sports and hitting the books.

Time had gone by so fast, I couldn't believe high school graduation time had arrived. It seemed like just yesterday when I was playing with my friends on the playground. My four years in high school had been just a blur of homework, sports practice, and spending time with friends. My life was like a movie that was on fast forward.

Unlike a lot of my classmates who were eager to leave the island, I loved Kodiak and everything about island living. One of my favorite things was the sunrise. The sun glows an incredible color as it rises above the mountains. The bright sunlight illuminates the local rivers and lakes, giving them a supernatural look—so bright, so alive.

There isn't a prettier place on earth. I can look in any direction and see a picture-perfect landscape. Every view looks like a famous painting. And the streams are so pure and untouched that people can drink directly from them. It's truly God's country, a place that I love to call home.

As I was leaving to attend my graduation ceremony, I couldn't help but get a little emotional. I turned to see my house for the last time as a high school student, as a kid. I knew that when I returned home, everything was going to be different.

I reached up to touch our family slogan hung over our door and felt strange. I'd tapped that sign a thousand times, but it felt awkward now. Mom had posted it there during my parents' first year in Alaska. It was a simple slogan that my parents tried to live by every day. The plaque had a picture of a cross and inscribed next to it were four little words: "There is always HOPE!" My mom had hammered that into my head every time I was frustrated with school or we lost an important football game. She often told me that if it weren't for those words, she might not have made it in Alaska.

I thought about our family motto with a smile as I marched out for my graduation ceremony. I'd survived the first 18 years of my life, but I knew my life would be different after that day.

I just didn't know how much.

# ~ 5 ~

High school graduation was great because my grandparents and uncle had flown in from Michigan. It was nice having everyone there and hearing the gym erupt when they called out "André Adam Brown II"!

A bunch of friends started chanting, "Dré, Dré." It felt like I was back at a Friday night football game under the lights. I'm sure most of my friends thought I would have some outrageous stunt planned, but I knew better. This wasn't the time or the place to do anything really crazy, plus I didn't want to do anything that would prevent me from getting my diploma.

When I walked off the stage, my friends weren't completely disappointed. I'd tied a bushy red foxtail on the back of my graduation cap when I was backstage so everyone got their laughs. I glanced at our principal, Mr. Smith, and he even smiled a little.

Afterward we went out to eat at my favorite restaurant, The Roost. They had all kinds of great food. Since it was such an important day, Mom and Dad let me order whatever I wanted. I didn't hesitate and ordered the biggest plate of fresh Alaskan king crab legs they had. When the waitress brought the plate, I couldn't believe how good they smelled. They tasted amazing too, and each bite melted in my mouth.

The mood was great. Everyone was excited and happy. I was proud that I'd graduated from high school and was also looking forward to the future. I figured there would be no shortage of adventures working alongside my dad on the *Lil' Carpathia*.

As we were finishing our meal, I heard clapping and looked over my shoulder. The waitress was coming towards me carrying a huge chocolate cake. The fancy writing on it said, "Congrats, Dré, on your big day!" The white, green, and brown frosting looked like hunter camouflage.

Dad stood up and said, "Can I have your attention, please?"

He has a real commanding voice so that when he talks, people listen. The side conversations faded away, and all eyes were fixed on him.

"We are so proud of our son, Dré. We have a special gift for him. This is no ordinary gift, so open it slowly," he said as he handed me a large envelope.

I shook it. It was light and thin. *Probably money* I thought to myself as I slowly opened the envelope.

A brown card fell out as I tipped the envelope upside down. The front of the card read, "Congratulations Graduate!"

I opened the card and started reading it aloud.

Dear Dré,

It has been our absolute pleasure to have you as our son. We have had so many great memories and know that God is going to continue to bless your life. We know you are excited to start working on the boat this fall, but we are going to have to delay your voyage as First Mate because this August you are going to hunt a Kodiak brown bear.

Thanks for being the best son! We hope you are ready for an amazing adventure!

Love,

Dad and Mom

I was so excited! I'd waited so long for my chance to tackle the mighty Kodiak brown bear.

There was only one thing stopping me from going on my dream hunt right then—summer. I'd have to wait three months for hunting season, and that seemed like a lifetime away. Waiting probably seemed harder because I was so excited.

We wouldn't be hunting until late August, so I spent many hours helping Dad work on the boat. If I was going to be his first mate, I needed to know as much as possible about the ins and outs of the *Lil' Carpathia.*

I was also determined to stay in shape and be ready for the fall hunt. I began running on some of the nearby mountains and tried to exercise at least four times a week. I knew that the brown bear hunt was going to be tough both mentally and physically.

I often took Major with me on some of my longer runs. The running really gave me time to think. Major and I encountered a ton of wildlife on every jog. One time we even saw a wolverine chasing a rabbit. It was amazing.

June quickly passed and before long July was gone too. August was finally here. I was in shape and work on the boat was almost finished for the fall fishing season. Our hunting trip was only a couple weeks away.

There was one question I'd waited all summer to ask my dad, but I was hoping that he would tell me the answer first. It was something I needed to know before heading out in the mountains for our bear hunt.

I finally worked up enough courage one day when I knew Dad would be alone on the boat making a couple last minute adjustments on the navigational system.

It was a late afternoon, and most of the other fishing captains had already gone home. This was my chance so I went to the boat and called out to him.

"Why are you yelling, Dré?" a voice quickly asked from under the boat.

"Sorry, Dad, I wasn't sure where you were. Can I talk to you for a minute?"

Dad must have known that I was serious. He didn't say a word, but I could hear him coming up the stairs.

"What is it, Son? Everything okay?"

I nodded.

"Dad, tell me what happened on your last brown bear hunt. I know it's hard, but I need to know the details. What went wrong?" I finally got up the nerve to ask.

Dad let out a big sigh.

"I knew this day would come. I need to tell you, especially with our trip coming up. But I'm not ready yet," he explained.

Dad's demeanor changed. He transformed suddenly right before my eyes. He wasn't the rough and tough fishing captain. He was a loving father, maybe even a little scared.

I'd seen a neighbor ask him about it once, and he shot him a look I'll never forget.

His voice broke and quivered.

"Now is just not the time, Son. I promise, when the time is right, I'll tell you," Dad said, adding, "and the time is almost right."

# ~ 6 ~

I wondered if Dad didn't think I was old enough or man enough to hear his story.

The last two weeks before the hunt I spent a lot of time jogging at different elevations. I wanted to prove to my dad and Mad Mike that I was in good shape and could handle hunting in Alaska's toughest environment.

I had a small calendar I'd bought at the local dollar store, and every day I'd put a big red X over the date. I had one day left, one more run before we'd pack up and leave.

I usually liked to run in the mornings but couldn't on this day. We needed to finish up some last-minute boat repairs. I could tell Dad was concerned with the condition of the *Lil' Carpathia.* Time had taken its toll on the old boat. And since he was bringing me on as a full time first mate, we needed to catch even more fish to cover my salary.

Dad could tell that I was worried about the boat too. He motioned for me to come sit down on the bench near the Captain's chair. He and I have had many serious talks about life in that spot, so I knew he had something serious to say.

"Son, I don't want you to spend any time worrying about this boat or the fishing season. It's been a dream of mine to have you work with me. It'll all work out. Remember, there's always hope."

There it was again—our family's catch phrase. Mom and Dad would both often refer to the plaque that hung high and proud above our front door.

I believed him.

That night Major and I set out for one last run. This time I was going to do six miles, a run that would take me around town and up the face of Storm Mountain.

Major seemed extra excited during the run. Maybe he knew adventure was in my future, and he was excited for me. We were just about to turn onto Majestic Road and head toward the mountain when I passed the local airport.

Something was out of place. Usually the airport is used for supplies and hunting guides. But today there was a fancy private jet there. It looked brand new and was painted fire-engine red. This wasn't an ordinary plane so I thought someone famous must be visiting Bolton. Maybe some rich doctor or lawyer was stopping to get supplies before heading out on a hunt.

The side of the plane read C-III. It sounded more like a robot than an airplane. Seeing the fancy plane gave me something to think about as I finished up my run.

Tomorrow morning when I woke up, our adventure was going to begin.

# ~ 7 ~

After a restless night of sleep, the day of our hunting trip was finally here. Mad Mike had flown in the night before to spend the night at our house and help pack the plane. He was a rebel, a crazy hunting guide who usually spent his time flying in a small Otter airplane.

He was well-known around Alaska for two things: First, he was the best bush pilot around. No one questioned that. Though he had a reputation for doing crazy things with an airplane, no one denied he had superior flying skills.

The second was his hunting knowledge. He had guided hunters who took some of the biggest bears off Kodiak Island in the past ten years. He knew all the great hunting spots and how to get to them.

I guess you could say that Mad Mike was sort

of a celebrity around Kodiak Island. He'd been featured on several T.V. shows with professional hunters. Although he was kind of famous, he never let it go to his head. He always knew how blessed he was and how careful you had to be when pursuing the great bear. In fact, he almost quit the business four years ago when Dad was attacked.

When Dad was in the hospital recovering, he had a long talk with Mad Mike and reassured him it wasn't his fault, that they both were stupid for going after that bear given the circumstances. He also convinced Mad Mike to stay in the guide business.

Mad Mike was like family. He and Dad had been best friends ever since Dad and Mom moved to Kodiak Island twenty years ago.

Lucky for me, not only was I about to go hunt one of the most prized and feared animals on the planet, but I also had Mad Mike who was going to fly us in and help guide the hunt.

As we packed our gear, I couldn't help but think we had too much stuff. We had gear for warm weather and gear for sub-zero temperatures. One important thing to know about Alaska, though, is that the weather can change from being calm and peaceful to blizzard conditions in minutes. We would be hunting over two hundred miles back in isolated mountains so I guessed we had to be prepared for anything.

"All set, Son? Did you pack everything we talked about?" Dad asked.

We sat down on the dock next to the Otter, which was floating lazily in the water.

"I think I have everything, well almost everything," I said as I jumped up and took off running back to the house. There was one important thing that I'd forgotten.

For my twelfth birthday, I received the best gift any boy could ask for. My dad surprised me with a big knife, and it wasn't just an ordinary one. It was awesome! It had a compartment in the end of it with all kinds of gadgets.

I remember the first time I opened it, I was amazed. It contained matches, fishing line, hooks, a small mirror, and a compass on the end—everything a boy needed or wanted. But Dad always told me to save it for our first bear hunting trip.

Looking back, I think he told me that so I wouldn't lose it or get in trouble with it. Whatever the reason, it worked. I kept the knife stashed away, waiting for this glorious day.

I rushed into the house and grabbed the knife out of my top dresser drawer. I went into my closet and pulled out a belt and carefully wove it through the knife sheath.

I was ready to leave with a new sense of toughness. I kissed my mom, and she hugged me and told me to have fun.

"Please be smart. Don't let Mad Mike get too crazy. I'll be praying for all of you," Mom said.

With that, I went out the front door, stopped, reached up, and tapped our family motto.

Now I was really ready.

I just wondered if these big, old Kodiak brown bears were ready for me.

# ~ 8 ~

Mad Mike turned the key and the plane roared. The sound felt good at first, but I started to get nervous as the plane took off racing across the lake toward the edge of town and the old fish factory.

As we picked up speed, I could see a certain intense look in Mad Mike's eyes. I turned and looked forward. We were still heading right toward the factory. I squeezed the armrest as the plane roared louder and picked up more speed.

"Do something," I muttered toward Mad Mike.

At the last minute, I could see Mad Mike slowly pull back the wheel, and the nose of the plane lifted off. We climbed higher and higher. Our skis gently brushed the roof of the factory causing a few shingles to fall to the ground.

"Yeeh-hah!" Mad Mike yelled.

What a way to start! We hadn't even left Bolton, and I thought I was going to die. I could see the headlines in our town newspaper, the *Bolton Gazette*: Mad Mike Crashes into the Old Fish Factory!

*And I thought I was crazy!* My antics paled in comparison with Mad Mike's. I had a feeling this was just the start of a fantastic trip.

We circled the town once, and it looked so small from the air. It was the only place I knew, the only place I'd ever called home. But in that moment, it seemed very small. Mad Mike turned the plane, and we headed southeast toward our destination, Terror Lake.

I'd always heard stories of Terror Lake. Most of them were just tales told around the campfire. I think having a name like Terror Lake kind of lends itself to scary stories. There were always rumors about lost planes and bloodthirsty, crazed animals. I'd never been to Terror Lake, but I always wanted to go there. I thought it would add to my hunting stories to say I hunted Terror Lake.

The other important thing about Terror Lake is there are lots of big brown bears. Most serious hunters like to hunt within a ten-mile radius of the lake. There are plenty of fish and wild berries, which provide a ton of food for bears and other wildlife.

Terror Lake was the bear hot spot, and we were buzzing in a small Otter toward it, ready for a once-in-a-lifetime adventure.

Everything seemed perfect. The sky was blue and the plane was cutting through the air with perfection. Thirty minutes into our flight I heard Mike lean over and say something to my dad.

"We should be able to get there before the storm," Mad Mike said.

*What storm?*

"I don't think it'll be a problem," Dad said.

I glanced at Dad.

"There's a storm coming, high winds and a lot of rain. Mad Mike and I plotted our course and timed it so we'd miss it. We didn't want to be stuck back in Bolton for the rest of the week," Dad said, trying to reassure me.

In Alaska, storms can be dangerous and cause a lot of damage. Some storms have prevented hunters from ever leaving Bolton.

I was a little more at ease knowing that Dad and Mad Mike knew about the storm and had discussed it. I knew Dad wouldn't do anything too dangerous, especially when I was on board. The actual hunt hadn't started yet, but this trip was already filled with excitement.

We flew for another half an hour when a strange voice came over the radio.

"Northwest shift in storm, heading southeast toward Terror Lake. Caution! High winds and pouring rain causing limited to no visibility."

We weren't going to miss the storm, we were flying right toward it!

# ~ 9 ~

"Make sure your seat belt is buckled tight," Mad Mike said.

I knew that wasn't a good sign.

"Red Fox to Mad Mike, Red Fox to Mad Mike," a voice burst in on the radio.

"Go ahead Red Fox, this is Mad Mike. Our coordinates put us about 45 miles southeast of Terror Lake," Mad Mike said.

"No go! No go! I repeat do not continue on to Terror Lake. Hunters are pinned in. Terrible storm. Change your heading and go due south to avoid the storm," the voice demanded.

*Due south?*

There was nothing there, just mountains and several small isolated lakes. We needed to get to Terror Lake, but it sounded like that was going to be impossible.

“Duke, grab the map and try to find some water big enough to put the Otter down on. We need to get out of the air and brace for this storm!” Mad Mike’s words were rushed.

As soon as Mad Mike saw the storm front approaching, he instantly turned his wheel ninety degrees back toward the south.

The playful, crazy pilot was dead serious now. He knew danger was on its way. The Alaskan sky is nowhere to be during a storm.

I reached back to hand Dad the map when a burst of thunder shook the plane. It rattled us so hard the map slipped out of my hand and went flying around. We were getting tossed about so much it felt like we were in a spin cycle of a washing machine.

I couldn’t believe what I saw when I looked toward the horizon. The churning clouds looked dark and evil.

“We can’t outrun it! I have to take the plane down now!” he yelled.

Within seconds the storm was on us. Thunder boomed and lightning flashed; the entire airplane shook. My heart raced—I hadn't been that scared in a long time. I was petrified and felt helpless, but there wasn't anything I could do.

"Hold on!" Mad Mike yelled as the plane rocked and jumped. It was raining so hard it looked like it was coming at us sideways.

The plane started its descent. What had once looked like tiny mountains and trees from our previous altitude now grew bigger and bigger as we plummeted toward the nearest landing spot.

"There's a lake right over there, at your two o'clock. It looks big enough to land on," Dad shouted over the noise of the storm.

Mad Mike turned the wheel slightly and adjusted our heading toward the isolated lake.

The cab filled with strange electrical beeps and noises.

"Brace yourself!" Dad yelled over at me.

I squeezed the armrests and started to pray.

Within seconds we hit! BOOM! The plane impacted the water with a big splash. I got some idea of how a rock might feel when it's skipped across the water.

Mad Mike quickly pulled back the wheel and the plane turned, sending the nose into and then out of the water. We continued our dangerous skid across the lake, each wave like a speed bump jarring us out of our seats.

Suddenly the plane stopped still, the chaos and noise replaced by peaceful silence.

"Whew! That was close," Mad Mike said with a sigh of relief.

I nodded my head and looked at Dad, who was obviously shaken up.

"Are you okay, Dré? Are you hurt?"

"I'm fine," I managed to whisper.

Mad Mike restarted the engine and headed the plane to the shoreline where it wrapped around the woods. He carefully eased the Otter into a small inlet surrounded by trees.

"We can wait here in the plane for the storm to pass, but we aren't going to make it to Terror Lake. Duke, grab the map; let's see where we landed," Mad Mike said.

Dad had to search for the map in the scattered debris caused by our rough landing. Eventually he found it and handed it to Mad Mike who checked his equipment and got a location reading. He scanned the map like an army general planning a covert mission. There were no jokes, no smart remarks. It was crucial for us to pinpoint our exact location so we could radio for our rescue.

Suddenly a strange look came over Mad Mike's face. Dad noticed it too.

"What is it, Mike?" Dad asked. It was the first time Dad hadn't called him Mad Mike in years. This was serious.

"I don't need the map. I know exactly which lake we landed on," Mad Mike said.

At first I was relieved, but that quickly changed when I realized that something still wasn't right.

"We're off course about sixty miles. This is Deadwood Lake," Mad Mike said with a glance at Dad.

Dad just stared out the window.

"Deadwood Lake, is that good or bad?" I asked.

Mad Mike coughed to clear his throat.

"This is the lake where we hunted four years ago—the place where we both said we'd never return," Mad Mike said.

Dad pointed toward an old trapping camp on the western shore.

"That's where the helicopter picked me up," Dad said. "I recognize the place now."

What are the chances? We made an emergency landing on the only place on earth that my dad and Mad Mike wanted to avoid—the spot where my dad had nearly been killed by a brown bear four years earlier.

# ~ 10 ~

The rain pounded the top of the plane for three hours. We were safe, at least for the time being. We sat silently in the little plane as the storm poured down around us. I think we were all thanking God for our safety. My hands were sweaty, and I had a bruise on the palms from gripping the armrest so hard.

Our emergency landing had been scary. But what terrified me even more was the fact that out of the thousands of lakes in Alaska, we happened to land on Deadwood Lake where my dad was attacked. It was the one place on earth I never wanted to visit. This wasn't how my dream hunt was supposed to begin.

Once the storm finally moved on, Mad Mike got us out of the hidden inlet toward the main shore on the outside of the lake. The plane idled in the shallow water, and Dad jumped out to grab the tow line to haul it in.

Mad Mike got out and started to examine the plane. He and Dad walked around it twice, each time stopping to examine the engine. After they talked, Dad nodded and headed back to the airplane.

"Son, we need to start unpacking the gear. We're going to be here for awhile," he said.

Mad Mike opened his door and started playing with the radio. The rough landing had damaged the plane, there was no doubt. That was confirmed when Mad Mike threw the radio receiver against the steering gear and shook his head.

Thankfully we had all the hunting equipment and essentials we needed to survive. We had planned on spending two weeks camping in the wilds of Alaska. That was still going to happen; we were just sixty miles in a different direction.

"The good news is we'll eventually be found. I know Jimmy C and Gus make this route through Deadwood Lake to drop supplies off at various hunting camps. They'll be looking for us. It's just a matter of time," Mad Mike said.

"Why can't we fly home?" I asked.

"The engine block is cracked. I can't repair it out here in the bush because I don't have the right tools. It's not safe to fly. The engine could seize up at any second. It's a miracle we survived," Mad Mike said. Then he added with a laugh, "Maybe that fancy red plane that was in Bolton will come to our rescue."

Mad Mike was always good at taking some of the tension out of situations. The three of us enjoyed a chuckle, and for a second I actually pictured the red plane flying out to rescue us.

We started unloading our equipment. Dad and I set up two large army tents while Mad Mike secured the plane. The first tent would be our sleeping quarters. It could handle up to ten people. We also unpacked and hooked up the small woodstove. Even though it was early fall, temperatures can drop quickly in Alaska. There was no doubt we'd eventually encounter some type of snow.

The other tent was our cook/entertainment tent. We called it the Lounge. It had a small gas stove and a couple of tables. In it we would eat, play cards, and relax when we weren't hunting.

"Dad, what're we going to do?" I asked.

"We're going to do what Browns do," he said. "We're going to hunt. Starting tomorrow we're going to try to fill your moose tag and maybe run into a brown bear or two. Our first priority, however, is getting a moose for some food."

It wasn't quite the hunt that I'd pictured, but it was still hunting. I just didn't think in a million years I'd be hunting anywhere near where my dad was attacked.

He looked nervous as we set up camp. His mind was somewhere else.

I overheard him whisper to Mad Mike, "You don't think he's still here?"

# ~ 11 ~

I knew that he was referring to the bear—the one that had almost taken Dad's life four years earlier. I could tell coming back to the spot where it happened shook him up. He came over to me, his head hanging low.

"Drć, grab a seat by the fire. We have a long day ahead of us tomorrow, and there's something I want to tell you before we head out," he said.

The fire was cracking and popping. We had shared many campfires together in the past and lots of campfire stories. But this time I was in for a different type of story.

"I never thought I'd return to this spot. I still remember most of it, at least the parts before I passed out. Over there is where the helicopter picked me up," Dad said as he pointed to the northwest shore of the lake.

"This is a bad place. That bear isn't like other bears, Dré. He's a man-eater, a killer."

Dad took a deep breath and stared up at the sky. It was getting late, well past ten I figured. It's hard to tell in Alaska because it stays light well into the night. During this time of year, it's only dark from about eleven at night to four in the morning.

We finally got a fire going and gathered around it to stay warm. The flames on the fire roared as Dad began to tell the horrifying story of what happened four years earlier.

"We were following a huge bear into this thick alder brush. We'd been hunting for five days and were chasing this huge Brownie. He was the one I wanted! We had only caught a glimpse of him the day before, but we knew he was huge. Both Mad Mike and I thought the bear would square well over ten feet," Dad said.

The setting couldn't have been spookier, at least that's what I thought. Then I heard a pack of wolves howling in the distance. The sound made me jump.

"That pack is pretty close," Dad said to Mad Mike who already had his gun shouldered and had started pacing along the edge of the lake. He was looking toward the mountains with concern on his face. I'll never forget the wolves' sound, almost taunting us with their deathly howls.

"They're a good two miles away, but we need to make sure to carefully store all our food and anything else that might attract them," Mad Mike said as he returned to the campfire.

Without missing a beat, Dad picked up his story from where he had left off.

"We knew better. We shouldn't have gone after that bear. The alder bushes were so thick and it was so foggy, we could barely see five feet in front of us. After tracking the giant for twenty minutes, we stopped to catch our breath. That's when we noticed it." Dad paused.

"Noticed it? Noticed what?" I was totally caught up in Dad's story.

"We were standing in the middle of a graveyard with caribou and deer carcasses everywhere. Tons of bones were scattered there, and we figured that many more were probably buried below," Dad said.

"It was horrible, the most frightening feeling in the world!" Mad Mike added. "We knew we were in trouble—we were at the bear's home base, after all. The next thing we heard was branches crashing. The bear was on us in seconds. Your dad didn't even have time to turn around before the attack came. He hit your dad so hard it knocked him into me, and I went down too!" Mad Mike remembered.

"Your dad reached for his pistol. The bear took his giant paw and raked it across his knee. He took another swipe across your dad's face, knocking him out."

"I got two shots off at him with my pistol before I blacked out," Dad added.

"The first shot hit the bear in the foreleg," Mike said. "The second just missed his face, taking off a big clump of hair from the top of his head."

Both men were intense as they relived the story. It was something neither would forget and something they never wanted to experience again.

"How did you finally get the bear off Dad?" I asked Mad Mike.

"After your dad fired at such close range, the bear got spooked and ran off. I pulled out my .308 rifle and sent a bullet toward the back of the bear, but I missed. It was the biggest bear I'd ever seen," Mad Mike said, adding, "still bigger than any bear I've seen."

"I'm just thankful to be alive, Son," Dad said.

I was thankful too.

Now I knew the whole story, but it made Deadwood Lake even more terrifying than when we first landed here. I was glad that I hadn't known the details of Dad's attack before the trip, and it was obvious why he had kept them from me. Now we were camping right where the nightmare took place.

I was just hoping we weren't about to relive it.

# ~ 12 ~

I kept tossing and turning in my sleeping bag. At first I thought I was restless from the near-fatal plane ride. But that wasn't it.

Maybe I was excited about starting our hunt tomorrow. But that wasn't it either. I'd killed plenty of moose in my life.

I was restless because of that bear—the bear that had almost taken my dad from me. Not in my wildest, craziest nightmares did I ever imagine we'd go to the spot of the bear attack.

But here we were—sixty miles off our planned course. It was strange, almost too much of a coincidence. What were the chances of everything happening this way?

Our family didn't believe in luck. We always felt everything happened for a purpose. We knew God had a plan for us always. Even in the dark days after Dad's bear attack, we could feel God's presence in the situation. But why bring us back to Deadwood Lake? I couldn't get this question out of my mind.

Dad and Mad Mike, however, were having no trouble sleeping. In fact, Mad Mike snored louder than any bear or other animal I'd ever heard. They both had turned in because they knew we had a full day ahead and they needed their rest.

The wolves were still howling, and I kept hearing all kinds of other strange noises. Although I could identify some of them, others were mysteries to me.

After a couple hours, I finally drifted off to sleep. Suddenly a loud noise coming from the woods near the camp woke me up. At first I thought I was just hearing things.

I lay motionless for a couple minutes. Nothing. Things seemed quiet so I started to nod off again. Then I heard some rustling.

Looking out the screened window of the tent, I could make out the shadow of a huge animal moving around our campsite. I could hardly believe how quietly it moved even though it was so big. I couldn't tell anything about it except that it walked on all fours, and judging by the shadow, it was big.

While it circled the tent a couple times, I was too scared to even move. The animal was so close I was afraid to call for my dad. I just lay there, feeling helpless.

Suddenly I heard a bunch of crashing near the firepit. It was so loud it woke Dad and Mad Mike. They grabbed their .357 Magnum pistols hanging near their cots.

I sat up and motioned toward the campfire. Both men tiptoed toward me, and Dad bent down to unzip the tent.

Both of them sprang from the tent with guns drawn, but they saw nothing. Whatever it was had gone.

When they walked around the tent with a flashlight, they found its track. It was definitely a brown bear track, and it was huge! Dad could fit both of his hands in the giant's paw.

Dad and Mad Mike looked at each other. They

didn't need to say a word. I knew what they were thinking. They had seen this track before.

# ~ 13 ~

Both men tried to act calm, like they weren't alarmed.

"Well, it's almost time to get up anyway. Let's start cooking breakfast," Dad said.

I didn't say a word. There was nothing to say. I was definitely having the Alaskan adventure I'd dreamed about. I was just hoping I would live to tell someone about it!

Our breakfast consisted of wild blueberries we found growing near the tent and homemade campfire flapjacks, a Mad Mike specialty for which he was well-known. The berries practically melted in my mouth, they tasted so good.

After we ate, we were careful to put the left-over food in bear proof containers and wash all the dishes. We didn't want to encourage any more visitors.

"Let's head toward Lookout Point and see if we can spot a big bull moose," Mad Mike said.

Lookout Point was the starting spot for all hunts. It was a clear high point on the mountain that overlooked three different valleys, one of them known for its moose population.

We started up the slow difficult trek through the spongy terrain. Nearer the mountain, it changed and became rocky and uneven.

It took us about two hours to get to the base of Lookout Point. I glanced up and noticed how steep the hike was going to be. The face of the mountain was full of sharp, jagged rocks. We stopped and took a water break before going on.

"Well, Duke, let's see if this big, bad football star is ready for a little hike," Mad Mike said as he winked at my dad.

I smiled. If these two old guys could do it, it should be no problem for me.

But as soon as we started, I knew I wasn't prepared. It was hard to walk sideways. The rocks shifted and fell as we stepped on them, and they were moss-covered, which made them even slicker. The first hundred yards I slipped and fell several times. I could hear Mad Mike and Dad laugh as they moved up the mountain.

I guess I didn't know it all.

Three hours later, we made it to the top. I was exhausted. When we got to the high point, I collapsed on the ground. Dad and Mad Mike exchanged big smiles.

"Don't worry; it's easier going down, Son," Dad said.

I hoped he was right.

We positioned ourselves against some rocks and started glassing the valley for moose. After about an hour, we finally spotted a few. It was a cow with two calves.

"That's a good sign. There should be a big bull in there somewhere," Mad Mike said.

I spotted another cow in the distance. Minutes later, I saw a bunch of trees moving near her. I looked through my binoculars and saw a huge rack smashing the young trees.

I motioned for Dad and Mad Mike to look.

"That's the moose we want," Dad said.

I guessed he was about two miles away.

"Let's go," Mad Mike said.

I wasn't sure how we were going to get down, but I'd learned on the way up not to doubt or question these two guys. I just nodded and followed them as we started working our way toward the moose. We had to go down with the wind in our faces, which made sneaking up on him even harder and more time-consuming. After two hours, we stopped for a short break.

"We're almost there," Mad Mike said quietly.

How he knew that, I didn't have a clue because everything looked the same as when we started down. We'd been walking for a long time in thick weeds and brush. I had no idea where we were but felt relieved that we were close.

After a fifteen minute break, we started to make our way up a small ridge near the bottom of the mountain. Mad Mike stopped us near the top and crept ahead to peer over the edge down on the valley.

He quickly motioned for me to come up. I crawled to the top, scanned the open area, and caught movement out of the corner of my eye. I took off my backpack and rested my rifle on it. I quickly lay down and took aim. I could see the huge black object in my scope.

It was a cow. I hoped we hadn't missed the big bull. It had taken us longer to get into position from Lookout Point than we figured, so the bull could be miles away by now.

"Just wait—he's here somewhere," Mad Mike whispered as he continued to scan the area with his binoculars.

We continued to glass the underbrush for any type of movement. After about a half hour, Dad poked me.

"There, Son, there he is," Dad said.

I looked to the north and saw the huge bull moose a couple hundred yards away. Getting him was a long shot but one I believed I could make. After all, I'd practiced up to two hundred fifty yards with my .300 Winchester Magnum rifle.

"I can hit him there, Dad," I quickly said.

Dad and Mad Mike both nodded. I turned and positioned my pack and rifle, facing the giant moose. There was no doubt this was a big animal. I started to shake when I saw his outline in my scope.

I tried not to look at the horns but couldn't help it. They took up my entire scope. I took a couple calming breaths and put the crosshairs behind the bull's shoulder.

"Take one last breath in and slowly let it out. Fire when you're ready, Dré," Dad said.

That's exactly what I did.

The sound of the gun jarred me as it jumped against my shoulder. I was sure I'd held it tight behind my shoulder when I fired.

"Great shot!" Mad Mike yelled.

I scurried for my binoculars and watched the big bull fall after running about forty yards.

I had a great Alaskan trophy, but even more importantly, we had food to survive the next week. In Alaska, we don't kill for trophies, we hunt to survive. It felt good knowing that I was providing us with food.

I set my rifle against a nearby tree and took my backpack off. We all had special meat bags in our packs and planned on packing out all the meat. We knew it would take a couple trips to get it back to camp, which we figured was about three miles away as the crow flies.

"That was the fun part; now comes the work," Dad said with a wink.

Field dressing this giant brute was going to be challenging, but this wasn't the first time for any of us. Both Dad and Mad Mike had butchered plenty of moose. They wasted no time as they started to skin the animal.

When we were all packed up to make the trek back to camp with our first load, we headed toward the nearby river. We knew that walking along the river back to camp would be much easier and quicker than tromping through alder brush. We also knew it was entirely possible we could run into a hungry brown bear going that way.

We wanted to avoid a bear, at least for now. We needed to get the moose packed out before worrying about bear hunting.

We walked next to the cold Alaskan water at

the edge. We knew we could make better time avoiding the thick brush and trees of the Alaskan landscape, and we knew the river would take us right to Deadwood Lake.

The hike was tough, but it was worth it to get my moose.

But we weren't back to camp yet.

# ~ 14 ~

We were about a mile from camp, and my pace was slowing. I was falling behind.

"Dad, I have to take a break to catch my breath," I shouted out.

He stopped and looked back at me.

"Go ahead, Dad. I'll catch up. I can see the smoke from the fire. I'll be right behind you."

Dad paused for a second, waved, and took off toward camp. I was amazed at the pace the two older men kept, but I needed a short rest.

I unfastened my backpack and found a huge, gray stone to sit on. The river sounded so peaceful. The slushing of the rapids almost put me to sleep. I was tired, that was for sure. After a couple minutes, I stood up to continue the journey. I didn't want Dad and Mad Mike to get too far ahead of me.

The meat from the moose carried a strong smell. I laughed at the thought. I was sure it could be detected miles away, it was so strong.

When I reached down to pick up my backpack, I saw movement behind me. The woods were suddenly quiet. There weren't any of the sounds that had been accompanying me just minutes earlier—not one bird was singing now. It was an eerie silence.

I squinted and wiped the sweat out of my eyes. I knew I'd seen something. I looked harder but saw nothing.

"I must be going crazy from all this work," I laughed to myself.

I took about ten steps and stopped. I turned around, expecting to see a giant bear or something sneaking up behind me. But again, there was nothing.

I stepped up my pace. I certainly didn't need Dad and Mad Mike to tease me about being soft when I got back to camp. Besides, I was getting a little scared.

I went a couple hundred yards when a terrifying howl echoed behind me. The wolf was close, very close. In fact, when I heard him I almost fell over in fear. The howl sent a wave of fright through me. I froze. My body was locked in place. I couldn't move.

One howl was bad enough, but more howls quickly followed. Before I knew it, four different howls headed in my direction.

I slowly turned and saw one dark, black wolf staring at me, motionless. Its teeth bared, it was giving out a low growling noise, calling for reinforcements.

I knew there was no sense yelling for Dad or Mad Mike. I figured they would have already heard the wolves and would be back for me any minute.

The first wolf was quickly joined by three others, all snarling and snapping their teeth.

The strange look in their eyes told me that they were angry and hungry. They edged out of the underbrush onto the riverbank.

I slowly reached back for my rifle. It wasn't there.

I'd left it propped against the tree near the moose. I was unarmed and alone.

At least I thought I was alone.

# ~ 15 ~

I looked toward camp and couldn't see either Dad or Mad Mike so there was no way that they would be able to make it back in time to save me. I'd be nothing but picked over bones by .the time they reached my position on this side of the river. It was up to me. I had to do something to save my own life.

The wolves slowly started inching in my direction. I scanned the landscape looking for a way out or even a tree to climb.

There was nothing. Instinct kicked in, and I knew I had only one option. I dropped my pack and threw it toward them.

They stopped to examine the moose meat. I thought maybe they had tracked me because of the overwhelming smell of the game in my pack.

My plan only stopped them for a little while. I

slowly started making my way toward camp, hoping they wouldn't notice me. I watched while one of the wolves ripped apart the pack and began eating the meat. They acted like they were starving, which was hard to believe with all the game the area had to offer. My backpack only slowed them. The big black wolf, the original one, started toward me again.

Now I was really scared, but it wasn't the same type of fear that I'd experienced during our nerve-racking plane crash.

The fierce animal seemed like it was moving in slow motion, heading straight for me. I know animals don't have emotions like humans, but it felt like this wolf was determined to get me.

He was starting to close in on me. When he got within about ten feet, I did the only thing I could. I turned and took two steps and jumped in the fast flowing river. I swam quickly to the center, its deepest part, too deep for me to touch bottom. Glancing back toward the bank, I could see all four wolves looking in my direction.

I'd jumped in as a last resort. It was either that

or become the featured item on the wolves' dinner menu.

But now the one thing I thought would save me could prove to be more dangerous. The river's strong current was flinging me head first toward the dangerous rapids that lie between me and Deadwood Lake. I had trouble keeping my face above water as the angry river pulled me along.

For just a second I wondered if I might not have been better off to get eaten by the wolves. But at least I was still alive—for the time being.

After a couple minutes of fighting the water, I managed a quick glance toward the bank. I couldn't believe my eyes! The wolf pack was following me along the edge of the river. These guys knew how to hunt, and they weren't about to be outsmarted by a human teenager.

I was getting closer to the rapids, hoping that Dad and Mad Mike would intercept my unwanted companions. My biggest problem was that the rapids were shallow with dangerous rocks just below the surface ready to smash my head.

It may have been my imagination, but it appeared the patient wolves also realized that I was heading toward the shallows and that it would be an ideal spot where they could ambush me.

My foot hit bottom. I looked up and could see the rocky, rushing rapids ahead of me. On my right, the wolves stood waiting.

I thought I'd be happy enough to survive the aggressive river, but I wasn't. I remained in the shallows looking around as the wolves approached me. I could see Deadwood Lake, and I could see the smoke floating up from our campfire on the opposite side of the huge lake.

Dad and Mad Mike were coming I was sure. They'd know by now that I had run into trouble, but it would take too much time for them to reach me. From my standpoint, the brutal terrain was so wet and soggy that it was impossible to run or get any footing.

Dad and Mad Mike were still nowhere in sight. I only heard three things—the rushing of the rapids, the howling of the wolves, and my heart banging in my chest out of fear.

Would anyone rescue me?

# ~ 16 ~

I pulled out my knife and braced myself.

If these wolves were going to attack, at least they were going to remember me. I picked up a couple of rocks with my other hand and heaved them at their leader, the black wolf.

The rocks had no effect. These wolves weren't afraid of me. In fact, they seemed to be trying to outsmart me.

Without warning, one of them broke from the pack and crossed the river behind me, near the rapids, while the other three circled me on the other side. They had quickly managed to surround me.

I crouched in a fighting position, something like playing linebacker on the football team. I was in a hitting position and readied myself for the initial attack.

It was strange. The other three wolves didn't do anything without first looking toward the large black one. He was the leader, there was no doubt.

Almost on cue, the alpha wolf started toward me. The others followed suit, slowly hemming me in. They had me trapped, and this time they were going to leave no way to escape. They had a well-practiced strategy.

One more glance back across the lake toward our camp confirmed that there was still no sign of help.

I yelled at the animals, hoping that a strange noise would startle them and change their plans. Another fizzle. In fact, it almost made them madder. The wolves were so close I could smell them. They had edged to within ten feet. I was in big trouble.

Then I heard a welcome sound, something I'd longed to hear—a gunshot. One of the wolves whimpered and took off for the woods. It had been hit. The original black wolf let out a bone-chilling howl, and they all took off.

My attackers were gone; I was safe!

I scanned the landscape, trying to find a clue as to who had come to my rescue. A large man emerged from the underbrush on the opposite side of the river.

At first I thought he was a bear since he was dressed head to toe in furs. He had a bushy gray beard that hung past his chest and wore what looked like a wolverine fur on his head. Around his waist was a bright red belt, and his boots had red laces.

He came toward me smiling.

"Hey, that was a close one, aye," the man said with a smirk.

I was still frightened and could barely speak.

"Th... th... thanks. You saved my life," I stammered.

"Let me give you a piece of advice. Never travel in Alaska without a gun," the man said.

I nodded my agreement. I didn't have the energy to explain about the moose hunt.

Within a few minutes, Dad and Mad Mike came running with guns drawn.

"Sorry, Son, we heard the wolves and came as

fast as we could. We had already reached camp when we realized something must be wrong," Dad said.

"I'm okay, Dad. This guy saved me."

I felt bad calling him "this guy." He'd saved my life, and I didn't even know his name.

"By the way, what is your name?" I quickly asked to cover my clumsiness.

"Clayton Bartholomew Jones III, but all my friends call me Cleatus," he said.

"Well, Cleatus, thank you," my dad said.

Cleatus nodded.

"What are you doing out here in the wilderness?" Mad Mike asked.

"Well, I'm a mountain man, one of the last true ones that I know of. I live off the land and sell furs on the mainland for money," Cleatus replied.

He quickly added, "But that's not why I'm here and not why I'm camped near Deadwood Lake."

There was a strange moment of silence as we all looked at each other with raised eyebrows.

Everyone wanted to ask Cleatus the next question, but we waited for him to tell us.

He stood proudly, smiling, just waiting and wanting someone to ask. It was obvious Cleatus wasn't around people very often. His behavior was a bit awkward.

"Okay, well, why are you here at Deadwood Lake?" I finally asked.

"I'm here for one reason and one reason only. I'm going to kill the legendary bear, Samson," Cleatus said.

"Samson?" we chimed in unison.

"Samson is a huge bear, one of the largest I've ever seen," Cleatus said.

"Why do you call him Samson?" Mad Mike asked.

"He's missing a large tuft of fur on the top of his head—remember the story of the strong and mighty Samson, and Delilah, the lady who betrayed him?" Cleatus replied. "It looks like someone took his hair clean off the top just like Delilah did to Samson. Only Samson the bear hasn't lost any of his strength unfortunately.

Everyone around these parts refers to the giant bear as Samson."

Mad Mike and I both looked at Dad.

"Cleatus, why don't you come have supper with us? We have a story you're not going to believe," Dad said. "You might as well call me a barber because I'm the man who gave that nasty old bear a haircut."

# ~ 17 ~

We got back to camp and had a quick bite to eat. Dad told Cleatus about his run-in with Samson four years earlier. Cleatus was amazed but didn't seem too surprised.

"I knew that bear was different," he said.

Cleatus went on to tell us how he had retired from some big auto industry job ten years earlier. He explained how one day he felt the city walls closing in so he sold all his belongings and bought a one-way plane ticket to Alaska. Without an immediate family to care for, his plan was to hunt and fish to survive.

"Boy, was I in for a surprise! The first year I bought all my supplies and headed deep into the bush on the mainland. I almost died that first winter. I wasn't ready. Alaska can be a rough place for a city boy," Cleatus said with a smile.

He added, "For the past couple years I've been traveling Alaska, looking for the biggest and baddest animals on the planet. That's what led me to Kodiak Island and Deadwood Lake. I wanted to hunt the ultimate predator, a Kodiak Island brown bear."

He went on to tell us how he had been tracking Samson for the past month or so around Deadwood Lake.

"That's one smart bear. I've only seen him twice. He's constantly on the move. I thought for sure I had him a couple weeks ago. I shot and missed. When he realized I was still around, he left. I haven't seen any sign of him until today. He has some hiding spot, somewhere where he can disappear," Cleatus told us.

With that, the four of us hung up the remaining moose meat to dry. Once it was unpacked, we headed back to my bull moose to get the remaining food.

It was strange walking past my backpack on the riverbank. Dad bent down and grabbed it. There were rips where the wolves had torn into the meat. The bag was in bad shape, but Dad didn't want to leave anything for the wolves to eat.

"They've had their chance," he said with a glare.

We packed up the remaining meat and horns and trekked back to camp.

I fell into the chair by the campfire. Mad Mike began preparing supper, and Dad and Cleatus were talking.

I stared into the fire. The red embers burned a majestic, evil glow. It startled me. I'd just seen that same red glow in the eyes of the alpha male wolf.

I never doubted that the wilderness in Alaska was fierce. I was lucky to have survived, and I knew I would never go anywhere without my rifle again.

I was starting to nod off when a familiar sound startled me back to reality. Howling! The pack was a couple miles away, but they were letting me know that this was still their turf. But the howling was different this time. There were only three rather than four. At least Cleatus had taken care of one of them.

I overheard Mad Mike tell Cleatus, “I haven’t seen a plane yet, but they’ll find us.”

He didn’t seem too worried about being found—at least not by people.

We had food, shelter, water, and a fire—all the necessities we needed to survive the Alaskan wilderness. At least for a couple weeks.

# ~ 18 ~

That night Cleatus entertained us with stories about living in the city, surviving as a mountain man, and his love for the color red.

He was an unbelievable storyteller, animated and energetic. We laughed for hours. I think part of the reason why he was so happy was because we were probably the first people he had seen in days.

Dad and Cleatus had a lot in common, and he was especially fond of the fact that my dad had survived an earlier run-in with Samson.

Before bed, I glanced toward the gorgeous mountains. Their snowcaps were almost glowing in the night. There couldn't have been a more scenic spot on earth than our Deadwood Lake camp that night.

"I wouldn't doubt if you all run into some

snow before this trip is over," Cleatus said to me as I was gazing at the mountains.

Snow? It was early for snow, even in Alaska. But since we had known before we left that the weather could change, we were prepared for it.

"I hope we do get some snow. That'll slow that old brute down," Mad Mike said.

"You probably need to think harder about what you wish for in Alaska. Snow would make for good tracking, but it'll bring dangers of its own," Cleatus said.

More danger? I didn't think that was possible. I'd already survived a plane crash and almost had become dinner for an angry pack of wolves.

The moose hunt was done. It was time to shift gears. It was time to hunt a brown bear.

It was time to hunt Samson.

Morning came fast. Even though I'd had the encounter with the wolves, I had a restful night sleep. I'd been so tired I didn't even remember coming into the tent.

I sat up and stretched. My arms still felt tired

and my back hurt. It was a lot of work getting that moose back to camp. I looked over and the other three men were still sleeping. Cleatus decided we were good company and asked to stay with us and help chase Samson.

I was surprised that no one else was up. I went over to Dad.

"Dad, let's go. It's time to go bear hunting," I softly whispered.

Dad rolled over and I could tell he'd already been up because he had his hunting clothes on.

I shook his arm until he opened his eyes.

"What? What is it, Dré?" he asked.

"Let's go hunting. Why is everyone still sleeping?"

Dad sat up on his cot.

"Dré, go take a look outside."

I went over and unzipped the front of the tent to poke my head out and look across the lake. I could see why they hadn't gotten up yet. A big storm front was moving in fast.

A few minutes later, it began to rain small drops at first and then great big ones. There were massive, dark storm clouds as far as the eye could see.

"There's another bad storm beginning, Son. We won't be doing any hunting today," Dad said.

The rain picked up and blew even harder. I looked around for some type of break, but I didn't see any. The sky looked almost as dark as an October night. The rain began to pound the tent even harder and sounded like a rock-n-roll band as it banged off the fabric roof.

I walked back over to my cot, disappointed by the delay in the bear hunt. Dad could tell, though, that there was something else that was bothering me.

"What's on your mind, Dré?" he asked.

I put my head down. I was almost embarrassed to ask. But I knew I had to.

"Dad, have you ever been really scared?"

Dad's eyes got big and he wiped the sleep out of the corner of his left eye.

"Of course, Son. Feeling scared is natural."

"Yesterday when the wolves were after me, I was terrified. I was so afraid. I felt helpless."

"Dré, anyone would have been. There have been lots of times in my life I was scared. Moving to Alaska with your mom was scary. When you were a sophomore and blew out your knee in football, that really scared me," Dad said.

I thought for a minute. Dad had not mentioned one of the scariest events in his life when he was attacked by Samson. He had almost died and was in the hospital for twenty-four days.

"What about when you were attacked?"

"I didn't have time to be scared. It all happened so fast. Son, I learned a long time ago that some things are out of my hands. There is a reason and a purpose for everything. I know someone was looking out for me that day," Dad said.

"But didn't it seem hopeless?" I asked.

Dad got this strange look on his face, almost like he was confused.

"Dré, there's always hope. Nothing is so bad or impossible that it can eliminate hope."

With that Dad rolled over to go back to sleep. As I sat there thinking, I knew he was right. Even in the darkest, most scary situation, hope is there. I had hope that I was going to be the one to bag Samson—not only to get a monstrous brown bear but to redeem my father.

I just hoped that I would live to tell the story.

# ~ 19 ~

It rained without stopping for the next four days. Being stuck in a tent with three older guys for four days isn't exactly a vacation. I was starting to get sick of playing cards and already read both books I had put in my pack.

It had poured non-stop for those four days. It rained so hard it was coming in sideways. The small tent felt like a tomb.

I was actually starting to get sick of hearing old Cleatus tell his stories. At first they were great, but a person can only take so many stories. Plus, I was beginning to wonder how many of them were real. Every time he'd tell one it sounded like a fairy tale, some far-fetched old man's dream.

He told us about his yearly trip to Africa to hunt lions and how he worked security at the

Olympic games in Atlanta. He said that when he retired from his job, he had made millions in the stock market and hadn't known what to do with all of it. So many of his stories were hard to believe, but they were mostly fun to hear.

Cleatus was someone who didn't have the appearance of having any money at all. He looked old and beat up. His clothes were tattered. He told us that he actually made most of his own clothing. I couldn't imagine anyone with lots of money coming to Deadwood Lake and trying to live like that.

I looked at Dad during one of his stories, and he looked at me and rolled his eyes. We were all getting sick of hearing Cleatus make up these tall tales.

Maybe it was the fact that we had been cooped up in the tent for four days, but we were also starting to get edgy with each other.

"This rain will keep pilots from flying," Mad Mike said.

The entire time we had been at Deadwood Lake, I hadn't seen a single plane. Now with the rain, we figured it would delay our rescue even longer.

Finally, at the end of the fourth night, the rain began showing signs of letting up. The four of us sat down at the table, and Mad Mike pulled out a map of the lake and surrounding areas. Cleatus showed us various locations where he had pursued the giant bear. We marked the spots on the map, hoping to find a pattern or a spot to start our hunt.

Cleatus had most of his encounters with Samson in two places. The first was on the river, the same river where he had saved me from the wolves. Samson had been sitting in the middle devouring salmon; but the wind switched and he caught scent of Cleatus, which sent the bear running in the other direction.

The second encounter had occurred near a mountain pass on the southern side of the lake. Deadwood Lake is surrounded by huge mountains, but the ones on the south side are the biggest and most dangerous.

Cleatus explained that he had been pursuing

Samson but lost him as the giant bear climbed higher and higher.

"I couldn't follow him; the terrain was too rough. For some reason that big old brute maneuvered up the mountain like he owned it!"

After examining the map for several minutes, Mad Mike spoke up. "We need to start here," he said. He pointed near the base of the mountains where Cleatus had spotted Samson.

"He's coming down to Deadwood Lake and the surrounding rivers to feed. But he doesn't hang around too long. He's smart," said Mad Mike.

Cleatus spoke up, "There's got to be a place he goes when there's trouble."

"I'd bet that if we start there we can find some evidence of the bear. We're going to have to be careful not to spook him, or we might never see him again," Dad said.

"Dad, maybe you should be the one to take care of Samson and give him a little payback," I said.

Mad Mike nodded.

"No, Son," Dad said. "There's nothing to pay back. He's just a wild animal and we're hunters. He isn't used to being the prey; he's used to being the hunter. But on this hunt, we are the predators. This bear is yours."

"Are you sure someone his age can handle a bear like this?" Cleatus asked.

"I have no doubt," Dad replied.

I was glad that Dad was so confident in me because I wasn't. I thought about my poor mom at home and how she would be so mad at my dad for even trying to pursue this particular bear. She would be furious knowing that I was the one who was going to try to kill him.

The skies finally began to clear. There was a sense of excitement in the air, a sense of hope.

I slowly chewed some moose tenderloin around the crackling campfire. I think I was starting to realize what it meant to be a man. It had nothing to do with being fearless or scared. And it had nothing to do with killing a bear.

# ~ 20 ~

We got up early that morning to pack for our trip to the southern mountains where we believed Samson lived. This wasn't going to be a quick day trip. We packed two small tents because we knew we would be out in the bush for a couple days. The good news was that we had plenty of food from my moose. There were also a number of small lakes we could fish in the valley at the base of the mountain range.

I had an eerie feeling as we hiked away from camp. The broken-down plane sat in the shallows. It was the only sign of home we had seen for the past week, and we were leaving it. We were leaving our safe zone to hunt a bear that had almost left me fatherless.

We walked for about four hours and sat down to take a water break. I was amazed at how the other men handled such a rigorous hike. I was a lot younger, but they seemed to handle it better.

"We still have another four hours to hike to reach the base of the mountain. Once we get there we'll set up our camp and start looking for signs of Samson," Cleatus said.

We nodded in agreement.

Cleatus was leading this expedition since he was the only one who had been on this side of the lake.

We could no longer see any remnant of our camp. The huge lake lay in the distance, and I could barely make out the brilliant blue waters.

The weather was changing; it was getting colder. As we got closer and closer to the mountain, we could see a lot of snow near the peak.

"The rain that kept us tent-bound came down as snow on the mountains. The higher the altitude, the more snow we'll encounter," Mad Mike said.

Cleatus went over to the edge of the ridge. He pulled out his binoculars and scanned the valley below us that separated us from the mountains.

A couple minutes later both Dad and Mad Mike joined Cleatus. I could tell they were having an important conversation. I didn't waste any time joining them, hoping to hear what was going on.

"I think we should go around it," Mad Mike said.

"We don't have that kind of time. You know that," Dad said.

"It's too dangerous," Mad Mike added.

"Let's leave it up to Dré," Dad said.

The group turned in my direction. I think they could tell I was eavesdropping.

"Leave what to me, Dad?" I asked.

"We need to go across the valley to get there," Dad said, pointing at the base of the mountain.

"Okay," I answered, a little confused.

Dad and the rest of the crew could sense I wasn't quite getting what the problem was.

"Listen here, boy. Crossing that valley is dangerous. The trees are thick down there. A lot of bad things can happen if we don't have the high ground," Cleatus finally said.

I looked closer and finally understood. They didn't want us to be in the thick valley with Samson. My dad and Mad Mike had made that mistake four years ago. Cleatus was a seasoned, experienced hunter so he knew it wasn't the safest choice.

"What are our other options?" I asked.

Cleatus spoke up. "We could take this ridge around, keep the high ground, and trek toward the base of the mountain. But it will add another four to five days to the trip."

We all knew we didn't have the luxury of that kind of time. We still needed to get picked up and didn't know how long it would take to get rescued from Deadwood Lake. And the longer we stayed in the wild, the more dangerous the weather would probably get. We didn't want to be stuck at Deadwood Lake with a broken-down plane when the winter season began.

Another important reason we needed to take the shorter route was that the local planes stopped flying their regular routes when winter came. We only had about five days left before then to have the planes spot our camp on Deadwood Lake.

"There's only one option. We need to cross through the valley. There are four of us. What could possibly happen?" I asked.

I had no clue about the danger that awaited us in the valley. No one did.

# ~ 21 ~

We started our descent into the valley from the ridge. As soon as we were down in the valley, I feared I'd made a big mistake. The trees and underbrush were so thick, it was hard going. I could only see about ten feet in front of me.

The only place we could make any headway on was an old caribou trail. The big beasts migrate through the valley every spring, and there was a lot of evidence of their presence. I was thankful they had made their trip because it made ours a little easier.

I'd thought trekking to Lookout Point was tough, but it couldn't compare to hiking through this valley. The bushes were thick and seemed to grab and rip our clothes as we struggled along. The ground was mucky and so it pulled on my boots. Every step was a struggle. I walked third in line so at least Dad and Mad Mike broke up the ground. Cleatus brought up the rear.

We were about halfway across the valley when we took a break.

"Let's start a fire and cook some moose," I said with thoughts of a hot meal pleasantly in my head. My stomach was growling already.

"No, that's not a good idea," my dad quickly shot back.

I suddenly realized why. I shouldn't have even suggested it. We didn't want to do anything that would attract Samson or any bear to our location.

We sat for about ten minutes and then started up again. After a couple hundred yards, Mad Mike stopped.

"Did you hear that?" he asked.

I looked around. I hadn't heard anything. In fact, it was dead quiet. I shook my head no.

"That's what I mean. It's too quiet," Mad Mike said.

Without warning, we heard loud grunts and twigs crunching in the alder bushes. The four of us crouched, guns drawn. Whatever it was, it was big and close. Within seconds we heard more crashing, even closer.

I spun with my rifle back toward Cleatus. He was alert and scanning the nearby brush.

Suddenly I heard a large rumble, and an animal was crashing through the undergrowth, running straight at us. I couldn't tell what it was at first. But it was in a hurry.

I pulled up my rifle.

"Don't shoot! It's a cow moose!" Cleatus yelled.

Whew! I exhaled a big breath. A large cow moose ran within ten feet of us. The underbrush was so thick we hadn't been able to tell what it was until it was almost on top of us.

"Stay ready!" yelled Mad Mike.

"It's just a moose," I yelled back.

"A moose doesn't run toward people unless—" said Mad Mike.

He didn't even have time to finish his sentence, but I knew what he was going to say. It wouldn't be running toward us unless it was being chased.

# ~ 22 ~

*Wolves? A bear?*

Whatever was chasing the large cow moose was a predator that had scared a twelve-hundred-pound animal.

The four of us stood motionless, listening. There was no sound at first. Just a quiet, surreal Alaskan stillness. But moments later, we heard it. It was a strange noise. At first, I couldn't tell what it was.

"It's feeding. The cow must have had a calf with it," Mad Mike whispered.

"It's feeding? What is?" I quickly asked.

"A brown bear, and it's a big one," Mad Mike replied.

The wind was still in our favor, so the bear had no idea predators were within a hundred yards of its location.

You could hear jaws snapping and a low groaning. Occasionally there was a roar, followed by smaller, less fierce snarls.

"She's feeding with her cubs," Dad said.

At least it wasn't Samson. I didn't want to meet any brown bear in this valley, especially Samson.

"Don't let your guard down, boy," Cleatus said, adding, "A mother bear is the most dangerous kind of predator on earth."

We slowly trekked through the muck away from the fresh bear kill. It seemed like the bear had used the thick bushes and nasty terrain to set a trap for the mother moose and her calf. One thing was sure, we were on the bear's turf.

With each step away from them, my heartbeat started to slow down. We couldn't get away from that mother bear fast enough. After about an hour, we stopped.

"That was close," Dad said with a sigh.

"We're lucky the wind was right, or we could have been lunch for that big Brownie," Cleatus piped in.

Lucky? I think not. Our family didn't believe in luck. We believed in purpose.

I felt everything happened for a reason and was meant to happen. Maybe this scare was preparing us for something down the road. Maybe it was getting us ready for an unexpected visitor.

We were close to the base of the mountain now. There was only about an hour hike left, and we would be setting up camp.

I took a big drink from my canteen and looked for a comfortable rock to sit on. I saw one a couple yards off the trail. I walked over and sat down. To my surprise, I sank right through the rock and crashed into the ground. It wasn't a rock—it was a rib cage. I jumped up startled and looked around.

Bones—they were everywhere!

# ~ 23 ~

The four of us looked around and couldn't believe our eyes. We were sitting in some type of graveyard! It was full of all kinds of animal bones. Some were old and really white, but some still had meat attached.

"We need to head toward that mountain and fast!" Mad Mike ordered.

We started to jog through the underbrush. We were moving so fast no one had time to talk or ask questions. Our hour walk quickly turned into a fifteen minute jog. We didn't stop moving at that pace until we had reached the bottom of the mountain.

When we got there, I saw a completely different danger. The massive mountain was incredibly steep and rock-covered. The chances of good footing were almost nonexistent.

"Let's camp here tonight. We'll trek up the mountain in the morning," Dad said.

Thankfully we found a solid spot to camp. There was a rock ledge about ten feet off the ground that had great cover. Plus, there was only one way in and one way out. The back of the mountain was so steep, no animal could come in behind us.

"We'll be safe here. We'll take turns guarding the entrance throughout the night," Cleatus said.

It was strange. We never mentioned Samson. We didn't need to. The four of us knew he was out there, looking for us, hunting us.

We unpacked our backpacks and began to set up our makeshift camp. Once the tents were up, Mad Mike started a fire. Dad unwrapped huge moose tenderloin from his pack.

"Do you think that's a good idea?" I asked.

"We have to eat. We can't be afraid of everything. It's just a bear," Dad said.

He was right. The long walk and excitement had made us all extra hungry. We would need all the energy we could get as we prepared to head up the mountain. But where were we going? Everyone knew that we would find Samson somewhere on this mountain. Now that we had found his hiding spot, his place of rest, there was no doubt he would be nearby.

What I hadn't realized is that we weren't trying to find Samson. This whole time I thought we were looking for a cave or perhaps the boneyard we had found earlier. I thought we were the ones hunting Samson.

I was wrong. We were the hunted. We were the bait, and Samson was the hunter.

# ~ 24 ~

"You better get some rest, Son," Dad said as I finished up the remainder of supper.

The moose tenderloin was fabulous, especially over an open Alaskan flame.

I sat with my back against the mountain. It made me feel safe and secure. I looked out over the valley we had just passed through and chuckled.

"What's so funny?" Dad asked.

I turned to him. "The valley of the shadow of death," I said.

"I will fear no evil," Dad said smiling. "Psalm 23 does come in handy at times like these."

"I'll take the first watch," Mad Mike said.

"I'll do the watch after him," Cleatus said.

We were going to rotate every four hours. I needed some rest. My bones ached and the blisters on my feet were getting worse. I stood up and stretched before heading into the tent for the night. Dad and I were sharing a tent, and Mad Mike and Cleatus were staying in the other.

I glanced at the men one last time as I headed to get some sleep. They were still telling stories around the fire.

Even with all the danger surrounding us, there was a sense of stillness and peace. But that didn't stop any of us from having our guns nearby, just in case. There was no way we were going to let our guard down with Samson lurking in the valley.

I was so exhausted from everything. Even the fear lurking around us couldn't keep me awake. The last thing I remember hearing is Cleatus bragging about throwing out the first pitch at Yankee Stadium and having a red Lamborghini.

I just smiled as I drifted off to sleep. The next sounds I heard were screaming and gunshots. Both Dad and I stumbled as we ran out of the tent. We grabbed our rifles on our way out. Mad Mike stood there with his gun too.

"Where's Cleatus?" I screamed.

Dad and Mad Mike were scanning the surrounding bushes looking for any sign of him. The noise and chaos were gone, replaced by silence.

"What happened?" I asked Mad Mike.

"I have no idea. I was sleeping and heard a loud noise. I heard Cleatus yell something and then heard his gun go off. He was gone when I made it out of the tent," Mad Mike said.

I went over to the campfire. There was no sign of Cleatus anywhere.

"Over here," Dad yelled.

Mad Mike and I ran over to a large rock that was perched about twenty feet from the campfire. It was a perfect spot that overlooked the valley. The only problem was that the back of the rock was exposed, giving Samson a way at Cleatus.

Dad held up a piece of Cleatus' buckskin coat laying on a big rock. There was no mistaking it. The garment was ripped to shreds. Huge claw marks separated the deer hide. There were also several large scratches on the rock.

"Bear . . . massive bear," Mad Mike muttered.

# ~ 25 ~

We looked down and there was a small, rocky trail that led to the valley below.

"Stay here, let me go look for Cleatus," Mad Mike said in a low voice.

Dad and I both watched as Mad Mike went down the side of the mountain into the valley. After about forty yards, we lost sight of him in the thick Alaskan wilderness.

"Now what?" I asked.

Dad looked around. He turned toward the mountain and then looked back below into the valley. He made a quick decision.

"Go pack up the tent and hurry," Dad said with urgency in his voice.

This hunting trip was teaching me a lot. One of the main things was not to ask questions. I hustled back and quickly packed up the tent. I moved to the campfire and started collecting our cooking tools.

"Son, we don't have time for that stuff. Grab the tent and your pack. Make sure you have your gun," Dad said.

"Where are we going?"

Dad didn't say a word. He just turned and pointed up toward the huge mountain that had protected us from the bear's attack.

Within minutes, we were navigating through the sharp, cut rocks. The mountain was so steep we had to walk sideways again. Every time I took a step, a huge chunk of rocks would crumble and fall hundreds of feet below us.

"Son, keep your eyes up. Keep them looking toward the top of this mountain."

After about ten minutes, we stopped to catch our breath. I turned and carefully glanced down at our camp below. It looked small from where we were.

"Dad, what do you think happened—" I started, but before I could finish my sentence, he cut me off.

"Now is not the time to worry," he said.

With that, we started hiking again. The farther up the mountain, the harder it was to breathe. It was also much colder. There were small patches of snow and ice. The rocks were getting slippery, and I was having trouble keeping my footing.

"Let's get to that flat spot, Dré. Then we'll stop and rest," Dad said.

A big flat area about the size of a football field spread out about a hundred yards above us almost like a plateau. Those last couple steps were agonizing as we made our way to it. Dad got there first, quickly took off his pack, and began rummaging through his stuff for binoculars.

Suddenly my left foot started to cramp, and I began to slide downwards. I reached up but had trouble keeping a handhold on the rocks.

"Help!" I yelled.

I didn't know if Dad could make it in time. He dove toward me and grabbed my right hand as it was starting to slip. With all his might, he tugged and pulled until I joined him atop the plateau.

"That was close!" I said.

"Too close," Dad said, huffing and puffing.

We both lay there trying to catch our breath. Our moment of silence was quickly interrupted by a deep growl coming from below us. We looked down and saw a big brown spot. Dad quickly grabbed his binoculars and confirmed that it was Samson—he was tearing apart what was left of our camp.

There was no sign of Cleatus or Mad Mike.

"Don't worry, Dad. He can't make it up the face of that mountain," I said.

"Don't be so sure," Dad said.

# ~ 26 ~

I started across the plateau as Dad stayed and watched Samson for a little while. I could feel the cold hard ground under my feet, and that was all that mattered.

Once I was a safe distance away, I stopped and took my pack off. I dropped onto the ground and rested my head on it.

Any energy I had was gone. I was completely exhausted and scared. It had taken us two hours to hike up to the plateau.

Dad turned and started quickly walking toward me.

“Don’t get too comfortable. He’s coming up the mountain,” Dad warned.

“What? How is that possible?”

We both went over to the edge of the cliff and looked down. Sure enough, the huge brown bear was slowly climbing up the huge face of the mountain on the exact trail we had taken.

"He smells us," Dad said.

I looked around. The wind was blowing our scent down the mountain toward the bear. This time we were in really big trouble.

Going back down the mountain wasn't an option, and it didn't seem possible to go any further up the mountain either. I couldn't see any trails. The mountain rose almost completely vertically in front of us. Directly above us was snow, and I don't mean a couple inches—I mean tons of snow, at least a couple feet deep.

Dad starting examining his gun.

"No more time to run, Son. This is where we'll make our stand. I've run from this bear for four years, and it ends today," Dad said.

Taking a stand was the only option we had left. We stood far above the valley, our backs against the wall. There was to be no running away.

We looked down toward what was once our camp. Sure enough, there was Samson. He was closer and moving pretty quickly toward us. I couldn't believe how fast a bear that size could maneuver through the sharp, slippery rocks.

"We don't have much time," Dad said. "Let's get our packs and guns and go to the back of this plateau," he suggested.

We took what we had and positioned ourselves. There was only one way in and one way out. The only way out for us was to go through Samson, or for him to go through us.

The three of us weren't all going to make it off this mountain alive!

# ~ 27 ~

For a second my thoughts strayed, and I wondered what had happened to Mad Mike and Cleatus. I could only hope that they had survived somehow. But there wasn't time to think about that now.

I had my own problem. A ten-foot tall brown bear was coming for us, and he was mad and hungry. There was no escape in sight.

"Come on, Dré! There isn't time for that!" Dad yelled, snapping me back to reality. "I want you to go all the way back to the end of this plateau and keep your back against the rock wall. I'm going to try to find a way to get above this plateau."

"You're going to leave me?" I frantically asked.

"I have to—there's no other way. If I can get

on top, I'll have a clean shot at Sampson. Then it will finally be over," Dad said.

I nodded. It was our only hope.

The snow got deeper as I edged toward the back of the plateau. It was only a couple of inches at first but was much deeper, almost over my knees, when I reached the back wall.

I looked up and noticed a high sharp cliff. There was nothing else. Dad had started to hike around the side of the plateau to find a way up. Just before he was out of sight, he turned and yelled to me.

"I love you, Son!"

With those last words, he disappeared in the whiteness of the snow-covered mountain. I knew I didn't have much time before the giant beast crested the mountain onto the plateau.

I quickly lay down with my rifle propped against my pack, using the same shooting position I'd used to kill the moose.

Dad was out of sight, and I couldn't hear anything but the loud thumping of my heart. It was pounding so hard and fast it felt like it was going to explode out of my chest. I stayed in position there for about forty minutes, waiting for some type of attack from the bear. Just when I started to calm down and my heart rate slowed, I caught sight of something through the snow.

At first, I couldn't tell what it was. But as it neared, I could tell it was the top of the big brownie's head. He was sneaking up to the plateau. It was almost like he knew that there was only one way out for all of us.

The giant bear crested the top of the mountain onto the plateau. He was about a hundred yards away but already looked like a giant. Once he was on top of the plateau, he did something I wasn't expecting—he stopped. Then he stood and stared toward me from behind a huge slate rock on the edge of the plateau.

I couldn't get a clear shot. His vitals were hidden by the rocks, and I didn't dare take a chance at just wounding him. I knew the only thing scarier than a healthy brown bear is a wounded one.

The bear knew something wasn't right as he

stared at where I was. I had the crosshairs on him several times, but every time he managed to move. I couldn't shoot.

The only thing between Sampson and me was open plateau and lots of snow. Once he cleared the rocks at the edge, he would be on me in no time. I remembered learning in science class that a brown bear can run up to 40 miles an hour.

The last thing I wanted was to have to take a head shot at him when he was charging me. Suddenly Sampson stood on his hind legs and let out a huge deep roar that shook my insides. He would soon be heading toward me. I was just about to pull the trigger when I heard a gunshot. The bear spun. It was direct hit. Dad must have had a clear shot.

I knew one shot wasn't enough so I readied myself for his charge. I couldn't see him, but I knew he probably had gone down on all fours behind the rocks at the front of the plateau.

In all the excitement, I wasn't thinking straight. I stood up and yelled above me toward where I thought I'd heard the gunshot.

Dad didn't answer so I yelled louder. Then I heard it. At first, I thought it was my dad yelling back. But it wasn't. I stepped out a little farther to try to see what it was.

Maybe it was our rescue plane. The sound was getting louder and closer. It wasn't our rescue plane either. It was an avalanche, and it was coming right toward me!

It was too late. I didn't have time to react. The last thing I remember seeing was a huge wave of white. It hit me so hard, I blacked out. When I woke up, I was covered in darkness.

# ~ 28 ~

Was I dead? I didn't think so because I was still breathing. I tried screaming but could only moan. It felt like I was under water, only I couldn't swim or break free. Both of my arms couldn't move much. For the moment, there was some air trapped with me in the snow, but I knew it would run out quickly.

My mind started racing. *Did the avalanche kill Dad? Was he still alive? What about Samson?* Maybe this burst of snow sent the wounded beast tumbling down the mountain.

But then another thought crept in. I could die. Even with all the other dangerous events of this hunting trip—being pursued by a giant bear, tracked by hungry wolves, and almost dying in a plane crash, I knew this snow was my most dangerous and deadliest enemy.

My air supply was quickly dwindling. My breaths were becoming shorter, and there was less air with each painstaking gasp.

I closed my eyes to hide from the dark tomb surrounding me. I wasn't really scared of dying. I knew where I was going. But there were still so many things I wanted to do. Then a powerful thought struck.

"There's always hope!" I thought about those words my dad had told me so many times and that slogan tacked over the door at home. Even in our darkest days, when things look impossible, there's always hope.

I took one last deep breath and said a little prayer and exhaled.

When the snow first hit me, I tried to curl up in a ball to protect myself. I wanted to hold onto my pack and gun. I couldn't see them, but I could still feel them in my hands.

I started to wiggle the fingers on my right hand, and they moved. I took another big breath and held it as I tried to shake my hand free. I slowly exhaled and wiggled with all my might.

To my surprise, my hand moved a couple inches. But the bottom half of me was immobilized, completely buried so there was no chance of reaching my hunting knife.

I kept wiggling and shaking my hand until a couple inches were created on both sides. From there I wiggled the gun and started moving it, creating a little breathing room.

I eventually created a small pocket of air about the size of my pillow by moving my gun and hands back and forth. I still wasn't safe, but it did get me some air and provide me with a little more time.

I couldn't panic. I knew if I did, I'd die cold and alone on top of this mountain. I just kept telling myself, "There's always hope." I was brought up to believe that no matter how dark the situation, there was light waiting to come in from somewhere. I believed it.

It was still dark, but I could feel around a little more. I didn't know how deep the snow was on top of me. I took my gun and rammed it toward the sky. With every thrust, small chunks of snow rained down on my head. I don't know how I did it, but eventually the gun was fully extended above me.

I tried to take another breath and couldn't. I tried again. Nothing. I started gasping for air. I'd used up almost all the oxygen in the chamber, and it was filling with carbon dioxide. I was slowly suffocating.

Now I panicked. I wondered if I'd breathed my last.

# ~ 29 ~

Suddenly there was a small light penetrating the darkness. For a second, I thought it was heaven and wondered whether I'd died and was being called home.

With the light came a little air! I could take some breaths again. With all my might I took my gun and thrust it toward the hole. Now the gap was about the width of a baseball, and I could see the sky!

The hole was about five feet above me, so I reached up and started clearing my way toward the light. It took me about ten minutes to dig toward the top.

Finally I could reach my hand entirely out of the hole and slammed it through toward the blue Alaskan sky. I could move my fingers and knew I was almost free. I was sure that if my hand could make it out, so could I. There was a part of me that was waiting for my dad to grab it and pull me to safety. But he didn't.

As I pulled my hand back down to widen the path, I heard a strange noise and stopped. My first thought was to start screaming because I thought the noise was my dad yelling for me. But just before I yelled, I shut my mouth. If I'd learned anything from this Alaskan adventure, it was patience.

The noise was getting closer and closer. It wasn't my dad; I suddenly knew that it was Samson! He had survived both my dad's shot and the avalanche. And he was coming right for me!

He was so close I could feel his heavy steps vibrating beneath the snow. His deep breathing was loud, and I knew he was looking for me.

Suddenly a dark shadow filled the hole and everything went dark again. The bear was right on top of me! For a second I was actually thankful for the snow. It was the only thing protecting me from the twelve-hundred-pound bear.

Without warning, huge pieces of snow starting

falling down the hole from above. Samson was digging for me! I was helpless and knew it would only take a few minutes for the huge bear's giant paws to reach me.

I positioned my gun toward the hole. I didn't know if it would work, but I did know it was my only option. Even if the barrel was full of snow, at least it would make a noise and maybe spook the beast off.

I pointed the gun toward the hole and slowly took off the safety. I knew the bear was only inches away from discovering me.

I shoved the gun up as far as I could, and the hole started to flood with light again. I could see a giant brown paw fill the chamber. The bear was so close I could taste his stale breath.

I slowly pulled the trigger. Click!

Nothing happened. The gun didn't fire.

# ~ 30 ~

As I'd feared, the gun must have gotten damaged during the avalanche.

The click startled Samson although only for a second. He stopped digging and took a step back. I knew even one gunshot wouldn't be enough to scare the massive bear away.

There was an eerie silence for about a minute. Then the digging started again, and Samson broke through.

The light hit my eyes and initially blinded me; but they adjusted quickly, and I could see Samson's massive outline above me. There was nothing separating us. I was face to face with the bear that had haunted our family for so long.

There was no slowing him down. I knew his next swipe would be at me, and there was nothing I could do about it.

I watched the brute rear up and stand on his hind legs. He was huge, blotting out the entire Alaskan skyline. From my position below, he looked like a giant skyscraper, the kind you would see in a big city like New York or Chicago.

Just as he was about to take one more swipe at me, I heard a loud, booming gunshot. It hit Samson hard and knocked him backward. I could feel the impact of the giant animal hitting the snow.

The first shot was quickly followed by another. I sat there motionless, listening. Finally I heard footsteps running through the snow, getting closer and closer with each pounding step.

Snow was getting kicked in my hole so I reached my hand up. I felt a strong, solid grip grab my right arm. Even though I couldn't see him, I knew who it was right away.

My dad!

After a couple minutes of pulling and digging, I was finally free. When I climbed out of the hole, I wobbled and fell down. When I hit the ground, I couldn't get up at first. My body ached all over, and I didn't have much strength. I was completely drained. I lay there and looked up at the sky. I'd never seen anything more beautiful in my life!

I took a deep breath and exhaled slowly. I wanted to enjoy the taste of the fresh Alaskan air. I exhaled again and rolled over to get up.

That's when I saw HIM! Samson was about ten feet away!

"We don't have to worry about that bear ever again, Son," Dad said quietly.

As soon as I mustered enough strength, I made it to my feet and we went over and admired Samson. We felt no hatred toward the animal. The brown bear is the ultimate predator. We always respected that.

Dad figured the bear would square over eleven feet, which was huge. I'd never seen a bear, even in books, as big as Samson. His hide showed years of scars and fights. Kind of reminded me of my dad.

Before we had much time to talk, we heard a loud noise coming from above the peak. Within seconds a small helicopter crested the top of the plateau. We were going to be rescued! The chopper slowly dropped down onto the middle of the plateau. I was even more excited when I saw Mad Mike jump out.

"You made it!" I yelled as he ran up to us.

"Of course, that old bear wasn't going to get me," Mad Mike said with a smile.

"What about Cleatus?" Dad asked.

Mad Mike put his head down.

"I tried. Found some blood but no sign of that crazy old man," Mad Mike said sadly. "I'll tell you all about it later. There's another big storm coming. Let's skin this giant and get off this mountain."

It was amazing watching Mad Mike and Dad skin and cape Samson. Because of their diet, brown bears can't be eaten. It's one of the few game species in Alaska that you don't have to pack the meat out.

"Hey guys, help me roll him off the edge of the cliff," Mad Mike said.

At first I was puzzled.

"It's Alaska, Son. Everything depends on each other to survive. Some animal will eat Samson and live because of him. That's how nature works," Dad said.

"And I have a feeling there are some hungry wolves around," Mad Mike said with a grin.

With that, Dad and Mad Mike quartered Samson and dumped the meat over the edge of the plateau. They took the hide and what was left of our gear and helped me into the helicopter.

As we flew back to our original camp on Deadwood Lake, Mad Mike filled us in on how, after looking for Cleatus, he had run into some other hunters chasing moose. He told them about our plane, and they quickly radioed their buddy who was fishing a couple miles away. The best part was that their buddy had a helicopter. So they quickly set out to rescue us.

When we got back to camp, we quickly packed everything. A big snowstorm was coming and with what we had just been through, we didn't want to stay in the Alaskan wilderness another minute. After fourteen days we were finally going home! We had a huge brown bearskin and a moose to take with us.

But even more than that, I was taking home so much about myself and life. It seems like when your life is almost taken from you, everything looks different. I appreciated things more. I was more patient and more thankful after the experience.

As we walked past the old campfire, my thoughts turned to Cleatus. He was a master storyteller, and even though his stories probably weren't true, they sure were enjoyable. He was a great man. I only wished that he was boarding that helicopter for home with us. I guess for him, this was home.

We soon took off. There wasn't much talking, no high-fives, just three thankful men returning home alive.

About twenty minutes out of Bolton the pilot radioed town. I will never forget the sight when we cleared the horizon and saw hundreds of people standing by the airport waiting for us.

I felt like a movie star!

# ~ 31 ~

The first person I saw was Mom. She was very emotional. I just gave her a big hug and told her how much I loved her. Everyone from town came out to greet us and see Samson's skin. The story of the bear had spread like wildfire, and the town was proud one of their own claimed the trophy.

We took pictures and smiled for our hometown *Bolton Gazette.* We were hunting heroes, but no one yet knew the price we had almost paid for our adventure. Our fame lasted most of the winter. We spoke at churches and schools and told how we managed to take a record-book bear.

The end of winter was nearing, and we started making preparations for the upcoming fishing season.

Dad, Mad Mike, and I were working on *Lil'*

*Carpathia*. We were hoping to get one more season out of her. She was in rough shape, but we didn't have the money to get a new boat.

That night I overheard Dad telling Mom that they might have to remortgage the house. They were both pretty sad since they had paid it off just last year.

"Well, Duke, there's always hope," Mom reminded him with a smile.

He nodded, but he knew it didn't look good.

The next morning, we all met down at The Roost for breakfast before working on the boat. The restaurant overlooked the bay, and I sat staring at our old, dilapidated boat, trying to think of ways to make some money to help fix it or get a new one.

Lots of boats were coming and going in the bay, getting ready for the upcoming fishing season. It wasn't unusual to see them stop in for fuel on the way to their fishing grounds.

One boat in particular caught my attention. I could tell it was brand new, the kind of boat every commercial fisherman dreams about. I wanted to know whose craft it was or the name of it. *Someday we'll have a boat like that,* I thought.

As it got closer, it was obvious how new it was. This was probably the first time it had ever seen water. You could tell it probably was fitted with every bell and whistle money could buy.

I squinted to try to read the name. As it came closer, the name slowly revealed itself—SAMSON!

In big red letters Samson was professionally painted on the bow. I turned to where Dad and Mad Mike had been standing, but they were already halfway out the restaurant door.

The three of us hurried down the pier as the huge vessel pulled into the dock. One of the workers jumped off and started to tie the boat up. Another went over to some of the other fishermen who were standing around looking it over.

The fishermen pointed to us, and the man headed in our direction.

"Duke and Dré Brown?" the man asked us.

Dad nodded.

"I was told to deliver this to you."

The man handed my dad an envelope, and he quickly tore it open.

> Hey boys,
> I heard through the grapevine you took care of that old bear. Did you think he could hurt old Cleatus? I told you that most of my stories were true. Wish I could be there, but I am hunting lions in Africa. Remember, there's always hope. I know you will enjoy your new boat. Hopefully we will have another adventure together soon!
> Your friend,
> Clayton Bartholomew Jones III (C-III)

"C-III," I said, looking at Dad. We both just grinned at each other, remembering the big red fancy plane we'd seen parked on the airfield at the beginning of our adventure. All his stories weren't tall tales after all!

Attached to Cleatus' letter was a title and receipt for the brand new fishing boat. The receipt said that it was paid in cash.

We now had a fantastic new boat, and better yet, we knew our friend had survived the wild Alaskan wilderness!

Our hope had kept us going right on through to a new beginning for all of us.

# About the Author

Lane Walker is an award-winning author, speaker, and educator. His book collection, Hometown Hunters, won a Bronze Medal at the Moonbeam Awards for Best Kids series.

Lane is an accomplished outdoor writer in Michigan. He has been writing for the past 15 years and has over 250 articles professionally published. Walker has a real passion for hunter recruitment and getting kids in the outdoors. He is a former teacher and current principal living in Michigan with his wife and four kids.

Lane is a highly sought after professional speaker traveling to schools, churches and wild game dinners.

To book Lane for an event or to find out more check out www.lanewalkerbooks.com or contact him at info@lanewalkerbooks.com.